HER BILLIONAIRE STALKER

EMMA BRAY

CHAPTER ONE

Devon

MY FROWN DEEPENS as I glance down at my Rolex and note the time. Fifteen minutes late. My secretary is fifteen minutes late again, which means that not only is she not here to get her ass to work, but I also don't have my coffee yet either. One of my number one stipulations, one of the most essential aspects of working for me, is that she have my coffee waiting for me when I get in to the office. Is that so much to ask?

Apparently so because I can count on one hand the number of times the bitch has managed to actually have my coffee waiting for me when I arrived, and even then, the shit was cold.

I sigh heavily and pinch the bridge of my nose. I don't have time for this shit. But I won't be able to function as an even halfway decent human being until I have my caffeine.

With a growl, I push back from my desk and head out the door. I swear to God, the chick is fired today. She can't handle even the simplest tasks. I shudder to think of the mess she's probably made in my filing system.

I hit a contact on my phone and then bring the device up to my ear. My man from HR answers on the first ring. I quickly apprise him of the situation before ordering him to put out an ad for a replacement stat.

I storm into the first coffee joint I see, the one closest to my office, and step in line. I work through emails on my phone as I wait for my turn to order. After five minutes of the line slowly moving, I look up, my scowl deepening. God Almighty, it's going to take me all morning just to get one motherfucking cup of coffee.

I go back to business, firing off emails to several members of my team.

I finally realize I'm next up in line when a sweet voice says, "Sir? What can I get for you?"

I look up from my phone, and all the breath whooshes out of my lungs.

The tiny girl behind the counter is staring at me from behind thick lashes. Her eyes are the lightest blue I've ever seen—like the sky. They're so mesmerizing all I can do is stare back at them for a moment.

When I finally pull my eyes from her luminescent orbs, I take in her little heart-shaped face topped off with perfect, puffy pink lips. Jesus, those lips are sinful. They're the kind of lips men fantasize about, the kind of lips you'd see in a porn film.

But they're on the most innocent-looking little angel I've ever seen. Her blonde hair is so light she almost glows like there's a halo around her. And it's not that fake platinum blonde coloring either. No, this is this girl's natural look. I just know it.

"Sir?" she prompts again uncertainly, her big blue eyes blinking up at me questioningly.

"Americano, dark, black." My voice comes out gruffer than I intend, and she blinks again, obviously taken aback by my tone.

She doesn't comment on it, though. She just turns to go fill my order. All the while, I can't tear my eyes away from her. She's dressed simply in a black long-sleeved shirt and jeans, but fuck if she's not the most erotic thing I've ever seen. She's not overly curvy. She's actually a little slip of a thing, but her hips flare out gently, and I can't help staring at the way they sway as she moves.

She hands me my cup of coffee and recites off the total. I wordlessly hand her my American Express card and watch her delicate fingers as she swipes the card. I'm captivated by every move she makes. Everything she does is beautiful and graceful—like she's poetry in motion.

When I move out of line to allow her to serve the next customer, I don't immediately take my leave. No, I sit at one of the little coffee tables that gives me a direct view of the captivating barista.

I place another call on my phone, this one to the head of my security team. "Yeah, I've got a new assignment for you," I tell him gruffly.

I suddenly need to know everything there is to know about this tiny angel that fluttered across my path.

Lacey

I hurry down the street, completely beat after a long day of work at the coffee shop. I know I shouldn't complain. I'm lucky the manager took pity on me and hired me full-time. So many of my coworkers are only working part time. Of course, most of them are in college too, and as much as I've always wanted to go to university, that's just not in the cards for me.

I mean, sure, I always got good grades in school, and my teachers always encouraged me to go the college route. When I was younger, I used to dream about being a doctor or lawyer—the typical big-money careers. The older I got, the more I realized that I really want to be a child psychologist. I want to help other kids like me who've lost their parents or who've been through some sort of trauma. Of course, that was until I realized the price tag a college education costs.

I'm an orphan, and as a child of the foster care system, I don't exactly have parental figures lining up to help put me through school, and I refuse to start off my life in humongous debt. Better to just scrape by and work an honest job than get saddled with a bunch of debt and a degree that I might not even be able to put to good use if I can't find a job in it.

I still plan on going to college one day—hopefully. But, I'll be paying for my classes upfront. Sure, it might take me longer to do it that way, especially since I'm hardly able to put back anything in savings after paying my bills every month. Seriously, it costs way too much to live in this city. Rents are out of this world, and I don't even have a car. Thankfully, I live close enough to the coffee shop that it's within walking distance, and I should just be grateful that I have an apartment that's even remotely affordable. There aren't many other eighteen-year-olds who can say they have a full-time job and their own place without a roommate. My place might not be as nice as the townhouses on Fifth Avenue, but it's clean and big enough for little ole me. I don't need a lot of space. I've never had a lot of stuff. Being shuffled from place to place will teach you it's best not to have a lot of stuff to lug around with you.

While it's not completely dark yet, the streetlamps are on, and I pick up my pace, not wanting to be caught outside all alone. While I don't live in the most notorious part of town, it's still probably not a good idea for a lone female to be caught wandering the city streets all alone at night.

I suddenly feel a prickle at my neck and have the overwhelming sense that I'm being watched. You know when you have that feeling that there are eyes on you even if you can't see them?

Yeah, that's what I'm feeling right now, so I can't resist the urge to glance over my shoulder.

My eyes scan the perimeter and even flit to the other side of the street, but there's nothing. Just a few other people bustling about their way, probably heading for home like I'm doing. I don't see any creepy pairs of eyes on me.

I shake my head and start walking again. I'm obviously getting paranoid. Probably because I'm so tired. People don't realize it, but working on your feet at a coffee shop all day is pretty demanding. The shop I work at is in a prime location near lots of upscale businesses, so it's hopping pretty much all day. There's really never any downtime. I'm always taking and making orders, but I'd rather it be super busy than super slow. When I'm busy, the time goes by fast.

There it is again...that uncanny sense that I'm being watched. A shiver runs up my spine as my footsteps slow, and I glance around nervously.

Again, I see nothing, but I still can't stop the sudden racing of my heart. What if there is someone there? What if they're just hidden in the shadows, waiting to jump out on me?

I hurry the rest of the way to my apartment and don't slow down until I'm safely inside with my door locked.

I press my back against the door and take a deep

breath, trying to catch my breath after I practically sprinted the rest of the way here.

I finally let out a shaky laugh and berate myself for being silly.

There's no one after me. I'm being ridiculous.

Still, I double-check my door to make sure it's locked and dead bolted.

CHAPTER TWO

Devon

LACEY. Eighteen. Barely legal. Way too young for me. Not that I'm old by any means. I'm only twenty-eight. Even so, that's ten years older than her. She's still a teenager, for Christ's sake. I should care about that, shouldn't I?

As I sit across the street from the shitty apartment she rents and my cock gets hard just thinking about her, I realize that I I don't fucking give a rat's ass about our age difference. I can't stop thinking about her. She's all I've thought about since her light blue eyes met mine in the coffee shop this morning.

I honestly don't know what I'm planning to do. I'm sitting in my car drumming my hands on the steering wheel, contemplating just what she'd do if I burst through her door, threw her over my shoulder, and carried her off with me.

Of course, I know I *can't* do that. Still, doesn't stop me from wanting to, though.

It's bad enough that I'm sitting outside her apartment like a psycho stalker right now. She doesn't have a clue who I am. Probably doesn't even remember me.

She has no idea about the man sitting right outside her apartment at this moment obsessing over her.

No idea that if I wanted to, I could just take her.

It's a sobering thought. What's kept someone else from doing exactly what I'm doing right now? Lacey is breathtakingly beautiful. She's probably got her fair share of men chasing after her, though thank God my contact didn't find any evidence of a boyfriend.

No, my little Lacey is all alone in the world. She's an orphan who's doing the best she can to make ends meet.

Little does she know that I'd give her the world. She'd never have to work another day in her life if she didn't want to.

I frown as I continue to take in the apartment building she lives in. The paint is peeling off the side of the building. The building looks old and decrepit. I'm not liking the location this place is in either.

My little angel shouldn't be living here. She deserves the best of the best. A penthouse suite. Designer clothing. Jewels. Diamonds. Anything her precious little heart desires.

This is insanity, I know. I've barely spoken to the girl, merely ordered a cup of coffee from her, and here I am ready to lay down my life for her.

But it is what it is. I've never felt such a potent desire for anything or anyone. She's like an itch I can't scratch. I can't get her off my mind, no matter how hard I try. Admittedly, I haven't tried very hard.

There's just something about her...I know she's meant to be *mine*.

I just don't know how to go about making that happen without scaring her half to death. I can't imagine she'd be receptive to a guy she served coffee suddenly showing up on her doorstep and demanding that she leave her world behind and come away with him.

She's already skittish enough. It's like she's already sensed that someone is watching her. She kept glancing over her shoulder nervously before she finally picked up the pace and hurried into her apartment.

I think of her little pink lips and imagine what they'd taste like.

I groan and palm my hardness that's pressing against the zipper of my jeans painfully. Damn, it's obviously been way too long since I've gotten laid if just the thought of the girl's lips can have me in this type of state.

I know it's more than that, though. It's just *her*. Everything about her. I need to get close to her. I need to be around her all day, every day.

I suddenly still as I realize a way I can make that happen.

I call my head of HR.

I think I've just found my new secretary.

Lacey

I've never considered myself one of the lucky ones. Good things just seem to find some people, but that's never been me. I've always coasted by and made the best of my situation, but I've never been the fortunate recipient of any stroke of luck.

Until today, that is.

I'm jumping to fill orders and keep the line moving as quickly as I can when a man in an expensive-looking business suit steps up to the counter and assesses me critically.

"What can I get for you, sir?" I ask him, hoping he'll make his order quick before the manager jumps my ass for the line getting too long.

He doesn't say anything for a moment. He just keeps staring at me with that probing look as if he's trying to figure something out.

I stare back at him, taking in his soft blue eyes and short blonde hair. He's probably in his mid-forties, and I'm pretty sure I've never seen him before, but then again, the faces of all the businesspeople who come in here blur into one as the days go by.

His eyes flick down to my name tag before coming back up to my face.

I stumble over my feet in shock when he finally speaks. "Are you looking for a new job, Lacey?"

I blink at him in confusion. "What?"

"A job," he repeats. "As personal assistant to my boss. He needs a new secretary, but you'll fulfill the role of PA as well."

"I—I—" I stammer, my head spinning at his unexpected offer. How do I even respond to something like this? I'm working as we speak. I can't think about this now.

"You'll be well compensated," he adds. He throws out a figure for what my "salary" would be, and my eyes bug out of my head.

First of all, I've never had a "salary" in my entire life. I've always worked by the hour and scraped by from paycheck to paycheck.

Second, that's more money than I make in five years.

I let out a nervous laugh and glance around the coffee shop, looking for hidden cameras. "Am I being punked or something? Cause this is totally not funny."

The man's brows draw together in confusion. "Punked?"

"Yeah, you know where this is all one big joke and then someone will jump out and pop my balloon once I get all excited?"

The man stares down at me like he's questioning my intelligence.

He pulls out a business card and hands it to me. "I assure you the offer is real, and my boss needs assistance right away. Today, preferably, so if you're willing, I'd like you to come with me so you can get started."

I gape at him. Okay, so maybe this isn't a joke. I

look down at the business card in my hands. *DeMarco Consulting*. My mouth falls open. I know that building. It's the biggest high rise on the street.

Mr. DeMarco is in need of a new secretary or personal assistant or whatever and the job is being offered to me?

"Why me?" I ask the question that's burning in my mind.

The man just eyes me. He doesn't answer my question. Instead, he poses one of his own. "Do you accept?"

"Hey, come on!" the guy standing in line behind the man I'm talking to complains. "Some of us have places to be."

The man offering me the job doesn't pay the guy any attention.

He's just staring patiently at me, awaiting my verdict.

I chew on my lip indecisively for a moment as my eyes sweep over the coffee shop.

I might have a chance to finally rise above this minimum-wage job. Of course, this guy could also be a serial killer, and I could go off with him and find myself tied up in a dirty basement. I remember the tingles on the back of my neck yesterday and the overwhelming sense of being watched. Was that the universe warning me?

I look up at him again and decide that I don't get creepy serial killer vibes from him, though. Not that I really know what serial killer vibes feel like, but whatever.

I remove my apron and toss it on the counter. "What the hell? Why not?"

The man's lips twitch and a see a spark of amusement light his eyes.

"I quit," I tell the gaping manager as I walk out from behind the counter and allow the man to lead me to the doorway.

Customers are complaining, and all hell has broken loose behind the counter as the team tries to reorganize and get someone to man the cash register I've just left.

"Lacey, are you crazy?!" I hear the manager's angry voice calling out to me, but I ignore it.

Yeah, maybe I am crazy.

But I'm going to take this chance and see where it leads.

What do I have to lose?

Not much.

CHAPTER THREE

Devon

SUNSHINE. My mouth tips up into a grin. Fitting that her last name is Sunshine when that's what she is. A fresh ray of sunshine. She's so pretty and pure, it's almost blinding to look at her.

Just as I'm thinking that, James, my head of HR walks in with my little ray of sunshine in tow.

And, God, my reaction to her presence is visceral.

My chest tightens, and every muscle in my body goes taut. I can feel my blood rushing through my veins.

She brightens up my whole office. I never thought

my office was particularly dark, but her light seems to illuminate everything, casting the rest of the room in shadows.

"Miss Sunshine," James introduces her formally, like I don't know very well who she is. I'm the one who instructed him to go hire her, to do whatever it took to get her to accept the position. If James was surprised by my sudden demands, he gave no notion of it.

I don't even spare a glance for him. My eyes lock onto Lacey's petite frame. Her sky-blue eyes are staring up at me widely, as if she can't believe she's really standing here.

The sentiment is mutual. I can't believe the object of my obsession is finally standing here in my office.

So close and yet still so far away.

I have to fight the urge to pull her to me and see just what it feels like to hold her tiny body in my arms.

James clears his throat, and I see him give me a stiff nod out of the corner of my eyes before he turns and leaves.

The door clicks behind him, leaving me alone with Lacey.

Alone. With. My. Little. Angel.

I grip the edge of my desk harshly to restrain myself from bridging the distance between us and finding out just what those puffy pink lips taste like.

She looks so young and innocent, yet the thoughts racing through my mind are downright sinful. I should be shot for the things I want to do to her.

Her cheeks turn a delicious shade of pink as I continue to just stare at her.

Somehow, I finally get myself under control and stand to introduce myself.

"Miss Sunshine, I'm Devon DeMarco. I'm pleased you accepted the job."

She licks her lips, and my eyes home in on the motion. I feel myself instantly hardening in my pants. My nostrils flare as I fight back a groan.

Christ Almighty, how long can I go without touching her, tasting her?

She lets out a nervous laugh and pushes that gorgeous hair back over her shoulder. I'm captivated by the way the sunlight glints and shimmers as it ripples back behind her.

"So, this is real and you're not a serial killer," she murmurs, as if she's speaking to herself. Her eyes widen, and her cheeks turn red with embarrassment when she realizes she just voiced her thoughts out loud.

I chuckle, raising an eyebrow at her. She's adorable. Completely adorable.

"You suspected a serial killer might be luring you

away with him, yet you went anyway?" The knowledge that she'd put herself in danger like that doesn't sit well with me, and my good humor fades, causing me to frown.

She shrugs. "Curiosity obviously won out over self-preservation."

I fight the urge to scold her for being so careless, because how can I really when it gave me what I wanted?

"I would like to know one thing," she ventures before giving me the full blast of those pretty blue eyes.

I look down at her, waiting for her question.

"Why me?"

Her question is innocent enough, yet I don't know what to tell her without laying all my cards on the table. I'm fairly certain she'll go running the other way if I admit to stalking her and hiring her just to get close to her.

"I was impressed with how you handled yourself under pressure in the coffee shop. I need a competent assistant. You fit the bill."

She nods, accepting that explanation, before she smiles at me. The prettiest damn smile I've ever seen, and the effect it has on me knowing that it's directed at me nearly makes me collapse. "Well, then, thank you for the position, Mr. DeMarco. I'm thrilled to be working for you."

Fuck me.

As much as it pains me to do so, I turn Lacey over to Maria to let her show her the ropes—although it doesn't really matter. Lacey can fuck up all of my files and make a general mess in my office and I would still keep her here just so she's near me. That's how bad I have it for this girl after one look into her pretty little sky-blue eyes.

I relinquish her into the hands of my capable office manager while I attend to important business calls throughout the day, though my mind keeps shifting back to her.

I glance outside my window every chance I get so that I can see her sitting at the desk positioned right in front of my office. My office windows are created with my private, yet controlling nature in mind. I can see out to what's happening on the floor, yet no one can see in here. It was an ingenious feat of engineering on my architect's part.

One that I'm extremely thankful for now as I watch Lacey run a delicate hand through her hair before she resumes typing data into the computer. I could sit here and just watch her fingers clack over the keys all day.

By the end of the day, I can't take it anymore.

I hang up my last phone call and tell Maria to cancel anything else on my calendar for the rest of the day. Normally that would be Lacey's job since she's my new secretary, but this is her first day and I won't throw all of that on her on her while she's learning.

Fortunately, Maria is more than willing to pick up the slack while Lacey trains, and there's no reason for Maria—or any of my employees, for that matter—to balk at anything I ask them to do. They're all well compensated for their services.

"Lacey," I call her name from the door of my office just as she's packing up to leave.

She stops mid-movement and looks up at me, "Yes, Mr. DeMarco?"

"Can you step into my office for a moment?" I nod my head at my door.

My eyes trail over her as she walks over. I don't step back to allow her entry, instead making it so that she has to brush by me to get into my office. She's so close I can feel the heat emanating from her. She looks up at me and blushes, her cheeks turning a pretty pink.

"Devon," I tell her as I shut the door.

She blinks. "What?"

"Call me Devon."

"Okay...Devon." She says my name hesitantly, and it's like I've been zapped with an electric current because I feel a buzz go through me from the top of my head down to the tip of my toes. Fuck, I love the way my name sounds coming from her lips—like it was made for them.

"Did I do okay today?" she asks me before she chews on her lip, looking up at me with wide eyes.

I realize she thinks she's been pulled in here for a reprimand for doing something wrong, so I rush to set her mind at ease. "You're perfect."

She smiles in relief, no doubt thinking that I mean she did perfectly when in fact I mean exactly what I said. *She's* perfect. Everything about her.

I gaze down at her, and she stares back at me, waiting to see what I've called her in here for. I don't beat around the bush either. I've never been a man who hesitates when he wants something. "Would you like to have dinner with me tonight?" I ask her frankly.

She looks taken aback. "Oh. I don't know Mr.—"

I make a sound that sounds something like a growl. I can't help it though. It comes out of me unbidden.

"Devon," she corrects herself before she finally

changes direction mid-sentence and asks me cautiously, "Like a business dinner?"

"No," I capture her eyes as I take a step closer to her and place a hand on her hip. "This dinner would be pleasure," I tell her huskily, meaningfully. I feel her tremble under my palm, and her breath hitches. I can see the pulse skittering away in her throat. The flush in her cheeks, and the way her eyes pool as they look up into mine let me know that she's just as affected by my presence as I am hers.

My cock lengthens in my pants, pressing against the seam of my zipper. I should just bend her over this desk and take her right here and now. The niceties and the dating and all that bullshit be damned.

I want to claim her in the most primal way possible. I want to see her virgin blood staining my cock. I want to take her bareback and come deep inside her pussy while making sure that I'm the only man who will ever be inside her. I want to nut all over her little tits and rub it in. I want to come in that pretty little mouth. Fuck, I want to mark her everywhere. I want to possess every part of her.

"I don't think that's appropriate," she finally speaks slowly. "You're my boss."

"So? I may be your boss at work, but after hours, we're just a man and a woman." My body heats with the implication. Lacey passes a trembling hand through that long blonde hair, and I watch it shimmer as it flows around her with the movement.

While I'm standing there mesmerized by her, Lacey takes a few steps back from me and straightens her shoulders. "Devon...Mr. DeMarco,"

I frown at her use of my surname.

"Thank you for the job, and thank you for the invitation, but I'm afraid I must decline."

I'm so shocked at the way she promptly shuts me down all I can do is stare down at her, still enchanted by her pretty blue eyes. Before I have time to respond, she's already turned on her heels and hurried to the door.

I watch her leave and can't help admiring how beautiful she looks even from the back, her hair flowing down to that impossibly tiny waist.

I smile even though she just turned me down. That doesn't deter me. If I need to chase Lacey and knock down walls, then I'm prepared to do that. She's skittish. That's to be expected, but this changes nothing.

She *will* be mine.

CHAPTER FOUR

Lacey

I'M SEETHING. I can't remember the last time I was this angry.

How dare he! How fucking dare he!

I don't know who Devon DeMarco thinks he is, but he can't expect me just to fall at his feet and put out just because he's my boss—and that's obviously what he thought if his manner in his office was any indication.

No matter that he's the hottest man I've ever seen. My skin is still tingling from the excitement of being in his presence.

With smoldering brown eyes and dark hair that a woman itches to run her fingers through, it's no wonder he thinks he's God's gift to women. But the man's audacity...

I snort, but then I sober whenever I consider how everything has come about. I got offered a job out of the blue, and I blindly took it without knowing anything about it. A shiver runs down my spine. Did he only give me a job because he wants to fuck me?

He said he saw me in the coffee shop...I shake my head. Surely that's not what's going on. I mean, who gives someone a job just so they can fuck them? If that was the case, he could have asked me out like a normal person.

But I already know as soon as I think it that Devon is anything but normal. He's *extraordinary*. Everything about him—from his obviously toned physique to his magazine cover-worthy smile and the Rolex on his wrist.

I did some digging on Devon DeMarco before my first day of work. I thought it would be good to know a bit about the company I was going to be working for as well as the man behind it, so I know he's a self-made billionaire. A man like him doesn't get where he is without hard work, determination, and perseverance.

As if to confirm my thoughts, my phone buzzes. I

look down to see a text message from a number I don't recognize, but even without a signature, I know who the message is from.

Unknown: Good night, Lacey. See you at work tomorrow.

I toss my phone onto my bed with a huff and then run a hand through my hair. It's no secret how he got my number. I may not have directly given it to him, but the man is my employer. He has access to all my personal details I provided HR when they hired me.

I blow out a heavy breath as the manager's words from your coffee shop I worked at just yesterday echo back in my mind. *Are you crazy?!*

Maybe I am because I just quit a stable job, and now it looks like I'm tangled up in one with an employer who doesn't take no for an answer. And he's set his sights on me.

I refuse to be *that* girl. The Office tramp. The one who submits just because she feels like she has to.

But I can't afford to lose this job when I have nothing to fall back on.

What am I going to do?

To complicate matters, I can't fully say why I'm so adamant about not dating him. Devon is hands-down the sexiest man I've ever seen in my life. Any woman would be lucky to go out with him.

Maybe that's the crux of it. He's *too* sexy. He probably has women throwing themselves at him everywhere he goes. He's presumptuous too, what with the way he pulled me into his office and acted like he expected me to swoon when he asked me to go to dinner with him.

It doesn't matter what my reasons are, I remind myself. He's my boss, and it's just not a good idea—even if just the thought of him makes butterflies take flight in my stomach.

"Why are you fighting this?" Devon's voice is low and husky as it fans against my ear. "Fuck, Lacey, your body is trembling for me."

He's not wrong. I feel like I'm on fire at his nearness. My body is buzzing and trembling without my consent. It's a traitor and doesn't know what's best for us.

He expels a breath right underneath my earlobe. The expensive scent of his cologne washes over me. He smells like spice and man. He smells so good. I have to fight the urge to bury my nose in his chest and inhale deeply like a drug addict looking for my next fix.

He doesn't deny himself such pleasures, though. He runs his nose along the column of my neck, and I hear his deep intake of breath. "You smell so sweet," he groans out before he goes in for the kill. "Have dinner with me tonight, sunshine."

Sunshine. It's an endearment he's taken to calling me. When he calls me sunshine, I know he's not just saying it as my surname but as something else. He uses it the way someone would use *baby* or *honey*.

"No," I deny him again. This is the same response he's gotten every day this week when he pulls me into his office like this and assaults my senses. He hasn't kissed me or touched me inappropriately. He's done no more than skim his nose along my skin like this or place a hand on the small of my back or my waist. He hasn't touched my breasts or pussy—despite the way my nipples harden and the muscles between my thighs ache with need.

No, he's patient and controlled. He's waiting me out until I break. He knows I'm on the verge of it too.

I don't know why I'm fighting this so much. My body does tremble every time I'm in his presence, and I can't lie and say it's from fear because I don't fear him. He might be overly aggressive when he wants something, and his tenaciousness is admirable, but I instinctively know he would never hurt me. No, the way this man touches me lets me know in no uncertain terms that he wants to worship me.

However, it's alarming how taken he is with me. We barely know one another. This must be an intense case of lust on his part because there's nothing special about me. He's at least ten years older than me. He's an experienced man of the world, and I'm just me, an eighteen-year-old girl who has nothing going for her except this job.

"Why?" He demands an answer. My brain is muddled from his closeness. His nose is skimming over my collarbone now, and the light sensation is sending snaps all throughout my body.

"Because you're my boss." I say the first thing that comes to mind. Yes, that's the reason I'm not giving in. It has to be because if things don't work out between us, I don't want everything to be awkward in the office —or worse, to lose this job because of a failed relationship. "It's not good policy to mix business with pleasure," I tell him. "Employers and employees shouldn't date. There's an uneven balance of power and all that."

He pulls back and frowns down at me. "You don't have to worry about that. I'll take care of you no matter what."

Despite myself, my heart softens at his words. He seems genuinely sincere.

As if he can sense me wavering, he goes in for the kill. He takes my hands in his two much larger ones and brings them up to his chest. I swallow when I feel his hard pecs underneath my palms. "Come on. Have dinner with me, Lacey. I promise you, nothing will happen that you don't want to happen." His brown eyes are like chocolate and just as tempting as they burn down at me.

But I shake my head stubbornly.

His frown deepens, but he doesn't release his hold on my hands. Instead, he uses the pad of his thumb to rub a circle along the inside of my wrist.

Goosebumps pop up on my arms, and my breathing becomes erratic. How the hell does this man know how to set my body aflame with the lightest and most innocent touch?

His eyes darken when he sees my reaction. Dammit, I can't hide it. I've never been good at hiding what I'm thinking or feeling. I wish I had one of those impassive poker faces—and that I could control my damn body.

"Is that all it is? That I'm your employer?" His eyes are regarding me intensely, searching for the truth.

I lick my lips, and his eyes flash down to them

before he drags his heated gaze back up to mine and goes on, "If I had approached you on the street and asked you out without this bridge of power between us, would you have said yes?"

I don't answer. I just look down, my face flaming because I know in my heart that I would have.

He hears my unspoken answer because when I look up at him, his mouth is turned up into a crooked grin, and his eyes are burning down in me. He shoves his hands into his legs casually, and I get an ominous feeling in the pit of my stomach. "In that case, you're fired," he says dryly.

CHAPTER FIVE

Devon

IN HINDSIGHT, maybe it was foolish of me to think that firing her would make her agree to go out with me. In my defense, though, I'm a problem solver. She said the issue was that I was her boss, so that logical part of my brain says to eliminate that problem. If I'm no longer her boss, there shouldn't be a problem. Right?

Wrong, apparently.

She looked both crushed and infuriated when I told her she was fired. She stormed out of my office without another word, amid all my begging and protests to get her to stay so I could reason with her. It took everything in me not to clutch her to my chest and hold her captive, but something cautioned me against physically restraining her.

Maybe I am a bit overbearing, but she's driving me crazy. I *know* she wants me too. I can read it in her body language. I can see it in her eyes. But she's holding back, and I'm about to go insane.

I haven't come since the first time I looked into her pretty blue eyes. I decided I won't experience release again until it's between her thighs where I belong. I'm wound up so tight I could explode at any moment, but it's not just the physical torture of needing release. It's more than that. It's a deep, emotional ache I've never had before. My arms ache to hold her. I would be ecstatic if I could just pull her against my chest without her protesting.

I call her cell phone, but of course she doesn't answer. I immediately call her again, and it goes straight to voicemail.

I harden my jaw as I type out a text.

Me: Lacey, please come back.

No response.

Me: You're not really fired.

Again, no response.

Me: Sunshine, I'm desperate here.

When she still doesn't respond, worry pricks at the back of my mind, so I pull up my camera feed to her apartment. Yeah, yeah, I know. It's a gross invasion of privacy. Ask me if I give a fuck. When it comes to my little angel, I'll do anything, and I'm completely unrepentant about it. I need to be able to make sure she's okay. I need to see her when I want to—for my own sanity.

I calm down marginally when I see that she's safely inside her apartment, but my heart twists when I take in the tears shimmering in her eyes. I grip the phone in my hand tightly. This is the last thing I wanted. I don't want to cause her distress. I just want to hold her. Why won't she just let me do that? We'll both feel so much better once she's in my arms. I'm sure of it.

I close out the feed to make some phone calls. First, I call a florist and schedule an ongoing delivery of red roses to her apartment every day. I know red roses are cliche, but they're Lacey's favorite flower, and I'll give her whatever she wants.

Next, I call a food delivery service and put in an order for healthy meals to be delivered to her door. It's been bugging me all week seeing the way she eats. Most of the time she doesn't get the nutrition she needs eating prepackaged trash like seventeen-cents-a-pack ramen noodles. That's going to change.

Finally, I place a call to my accountant. I'm going to make sure she's taken care of and doesn't have to worry about money ever again.

I'm going to fix this. I have to because I can't stand the thought that she's upset—especially since I'm the cause.

I have to break down her barriers because being without her is not an option I'm willing to settle for. I need her more than I need my next breath. It should scare me how intense my obsession for Lacey is, but I'm too far gone to feel fear. All I feel is need that burns me from the inside out. It's more than just physical desire. I want to possess her. Heart, mind, body, and soul. And I won't stop until I get what I want.

***

Lacey

I roll my eyes when a carrier delivers red roses to my door, though my heart does a little flip at the sight of them. The card is signed simply "D."

I suppose the spiteful thing to do would be to throw them out, but they're too pretty to do that to. It's not the roses' fault that my employer is a pompous ass.

No sooner do I finish getting them arranged in a vase is there a knock at my door again. My brow furrows as I sign for the delivery. I know I didn't order anything, but the delivery guy is insistent the packages are for me, so to make his life easier, I sign for them.

I frown when I open the boxes to find freshly prepped gourmet meals. "What the hell?"

Next, my phone dings. I pull it out of my pocket and swipe up to check the notification.

My mouth drops open. It's from my bank notifying me that hundreds of thousands of dollars have just been deposited into my account.

"Unbelievable," I mutter. I know exactly who put that money there. The only man with enough pull to meddle with people's personal finances without them knowing about it.

I pick up my phone to shoot Devon an angry text.

Me: Take your money back. I don't need it.

Devon hits me back immediately.

Bane of My Existence: Yes, you do.

As the name I programmed for him flashes across

the screen, I grit my teeth because he's right. I'd be a fool to turn down this kind of cash, but I refuse to accept it.

Me: I don't want it. The food either.

Bane of My Existence: I don't care. I'm not taking it back. Any of it.

Me: I can feed myself.

Bane of My Existence: Just eat the goddamned food, Lacey.

Me: I can't be bought.

My phone rings, and I answer it with a huff.

"I wasn't implying that. I'm just trying to take care of you. Please let me. Do you like the roses?"

It's the *please* that gives me pause. Something about the pleading tone to his voice catches me off guard.

"Why are you doing this?" I whisper.

"Because you're mine," he answers as if it's as simple as that.

"I'm not yours," I counter with confusion.

"Oh, but, sweetheart, you are. You just don't know it yet."

I swallow, my cheeks flaming at his words even though I'm sitting in my empty apartment all alone.

"Let me take you to dinner tonight."

I press a hand over my face and close my eyes. He's never going to stop. Devon has been persistent all week, and I'm starting to crumble. What could one dinner really hurt anyway? Maybe I am being ridiculous. I finally say weakly, "Do I have a choice?"

He leaps onto my comment like a dog with a bone. "I'll pick you up at eight."

The line clicks off like he's afraid I'll change my mind if he gives me enough time. Never mind the fact that I could text him, but knowing him, he'll turn his notifications off so he can justify saying he didn't see it if I try to back out of it.

Just to test my theory, I send him a text asking him what I should wear.

The text fails to go through.

I let out an incredulous laugh before I shake my head and walk over to my closet to get ready.

It seems Devon has finally broken me down.

CHAPTER SIX

Devon

I SEE LACEY'S TEXT, but I don't answer it until I can see on my live video that she's actually getting ready.

She's brushed her long hair until it shines, and my throat goes dry when I see the black lace bra and panties that she has on.

I send her a text.

Me: Wear the red.

I watch her closely as she picks up her phone and reads the text. Her eyes go wide, and she looks all around her before her gaze turns angry. She taps her phone and then holds it up to her ear.

My phone rings a second later. I barely get my warm hello out before she lands into me. "Are you stalking me?"

I don't even try to deny it. Instead, I speak to her calmly. "You asked what you should wear. I prefer the red one. It looks beautiful with your blonde hair and blue eyes."

I watch her little chest move up and down as she closes her eyes and takes in a deep breath. "You are unbelievable. Did you put cameras up in my place?"

"I—"

She cuts me off with, "No, you've gone too far this time. I appreciate you giving me a job, but then you hounded me all week until I agreed to this dinner that I told you I didn't think was a good idea due to the nature of our relationship."

"And I rectified that," I grind out, my patience wearing thin. "You all but admitted yourself that were I not your employer, you would go out with me, so we're no longer in an employer-employee relationship."

"So, I am still fired?" she quips back.

I growl and pinch the bridge of my nose. "No, I don't want you fired. I want you to come into the office every day where I can continue to watch you."

She gasps again.

Yeah, it's probably not the best time to spill the beans that I watch her in the office too, but fuck it. I'm laying all my cards on the table. She's mine, and she might as well get used to it.

"You watch me at work too? How? Are there cameras up there too?"

When I don't answer, she prompts me again, her voice shrill. "How, Devon?"

I sigh heavily. "The windows in my office. They're one-way mirrors."

"Unbelievable," she mutters again. "Normal rules of society. You just don't think they apply to you, do you?" Her voice is dripping with sarcasm, and I frown at her tone. She shakes her head and begins pacing around her room. I can't help admiring the view of her pretty ass walking in those little lacy panties. I fight back a groan, knowing now's not the time to express my appreciation of her physique.

"What I don't get is why. Why me? Why did you just offer me a job out of nowhere? Why are you so insistent on going on a date with me? Is this all just some misogynist thing? You're not used to women telling you no? You enjoy the chase?"

I grit my teeth. I don't like the implication in her tone. "That's not it at all," I tell her sternly. "I've never felt about any woman the way I do you."

"When did you see me? What sparked this...this..." She struggles for the right word.

I don't wait for her to find it. "At the coffee shop. You served me. That's the first time I saw you, and that's when I decided I wanted to be near you. I was already looking for a new secretary anyway. It seemed like a win-win. I'd get you out of that hellhole and give you a better job, and you'd be closer to me. What's wrong with that, Lacey? What did I do that's so wrong?"

She pauses before her voice comes out slowly, like she's trying to work through it herself as she speaks. "There are a million things wrong with that. So, what? You just saw me in a coffee shop and decided you wanted to bang me and instead of asking me out like a normal person, this is your way of going about it? Oh my God." Her eyes widen as comprehension finally dawns on her. "It was you. You're the one I've felt watching me. How long, Devon? How long have you been stalking me?"

"I don't just want to fuck you, Lacey." I grit out, my hand gripping the phone so tightly I'm surprised I don't shatter the fucker.

She scoffs. "Don't tell me. One look into my eyes and you fell madly, obsessively in love?"

"That's exactly what the fuck happened," I snap automatically.

She blinks, surprised by my outburst. Hell, I'm a little surprised by it too, but the admission settles over me with finality. I straighten my shoulders and own my words. Yes, that's exactly what happened. It might sound like some fairy tale nonsense, but it was love at first sight for me. "Call it love. Call it obsession. Call it whatever you will, but I want you, Lacey—more than I've ever wanted anything in my entire life."

She shakes her head. "You're a psycho."

"I would never hurt you," I tell her firmly. "You know that. I know you do."

I can't bear the thought that she might fear me. She runs a hand through her hair, and I watch as it ripples over her shoulders before she shakes her head. "No, Devon. This isn't love. Obsession maybe, but you don't manipulate the people you claim to love into doing what you want for your own selfish reasons."

"How is it selfish of me to want to keep you and take care of you?" I bite out in frustration.

"How do I know you'll want anything to do with me after you fuck me?"

My balls tighten up when she says "fuck me."

"Because, Lacey, I don't want to just fuck you. Yes, I want to see your blood staining my cock and know that I'm the only man who's ever been inside you, but I also want to climb so deep inside you they'll never be room for another man. I want to break your virgin cunt in so good that there'll be an imprint of me inside you."

I hear her sharp intake of breath. "How do you know—?"

I cut her off. "I know everything about you. I know you're a virgin. I know you're an orphan. I know you can't sleep with socks on because they make your feet hot. I want to know *everything* about you, Lacey."

She stands there with a dazed look on her face. "And," I add softly, "I also know exactly how to give you pleasure. I promise when you give yourself to me, you won't regret it, sunshine."

There's a long moment of silence on the other end of the line before Lacey finally shakes her head as if she's snapping herself out of whatever trance she was in. "I think I will wear the red dress," she finally says.

My shoulders relax. I'm glad she's finally seeing reason. Maybe she's finally realized there's no use fighting this. She feels this thing between us, too. I know she does. "I'm glad—" I began, but she cuts me off.

"I'm going out tonight, Devon, but not with you. Don't bother coming by."

"Lacey," I growl her name in warning, but she hangs up on me.

I call her back, grinding my molars together when she just watches the phone ring and starts getting dressed.

She doesn't know where the camera is, so she doesn't know where to point, but she holds up her middle finger as she grabs her purse and goes flouncing out the door.

She leaves her phone laying on the bed.

"Fuck!" I roar as I head out my own door to go track her down.

CHAPTER SEVEN

Lacey

I PURPOSEFULLY LEFT my phone back at my apartment. I'm pretty sure that if Devon bugged my apartment, then he installed a tracker on my phone, too. I don't know when he would have done it, but I don't know when he bugged my apartment, either.

Who knows? The man could have been slipping into my bedroom and watching me sleep. That should creep me out way more than it does. No, what concerns me is the way my heart flutters at the thought that he cares enough to watch me sleep.

But whoa, stop right there. Just because he watches you sleep doesn't mean that he cares about you.

He invaded my privacy in every way. He's stalking me. So what if he's a handsome billionaire? That doesn't make it right. Still, I guess I don't feel fear because I can't shake the notion that he would never hurt me. I'm more upset at the point of the matter than anything else.

I hail a taxi and have him take me to the nearest club. Even if I'm not legally old enough to drink yet, I am old enough to get into a club. I've never gone clubbing before, but I'm all dressed up, and maybe I just need to let my hair down and dance with some random strangers to let loose and work off some of this tension that Devon has built up inside me.

When I get inside the club, the music is blaring, and lights are flashing. It's definitely a fun vibe, and it's so crowded, it'll be easy to get lost in the crowd and become anonymous—which is exactly what I want.

I make my way onto the dance floor near a group of girls. They smile and welcome me into their midst warmly. No introductions are needed. We're all just a bunch of girls dancing together.

I sway with the music and try my best not to think of Devon. I try not to think of how he oversteps every normal human boundary. I try not to think about how it doesn't bother me as much as it should. I try not to think about how I'd feel if he actually listens to me and backs off.

I still haven't fully succeeded in not thinking about him when I suddenly feel hands on my waist.

I turn and look up to find an attractive blonde-headed man smiling down at me. He's obviously of legal drinking age because I can smell the booze emanating from him.

As attractive as he is, I'm just not interested. That's not what I came here for.

I pull away from him, but his hands tighten on my waist. "Where are you going, babe?"

Before I can answer, the man is suddenly jerked back from me. A fist smashes into his face. I gasp and look up to see Devon's eyes flashing fire. He looks downright murderous. "Don't ever put your fucking hands on her."

People have formed a circle around us to watch all the commotion. Devon grabs my arm and begins marching me off the dance floor.

"Devon!" I protest and pull against him, outraged by his behavior. He stops so suddenly that I slam into him.

His gaze is furious when he looks down at me. "Not a fucking word, Lacey."

I ignore him, of course, and yank my hand out of this hold. "How did you find me?" I hiss at him.

"It's my fucking club." He drops the words on me like a bomb, and my mouth falls open. I'm stunned and speechless, frozen in shock and unable to move or do anything. He takes the opportunity to fling me over his shoulder. His hands smash down over the end of my dress to keep it from flashing my ass to the entire floor.

People must obviously know he's the club owner because no guards rushed over when he punched the man, and likewise nobody rushes over to help me now when he carries me off the dance floor and up the stairs to his office like a sack of potatoes.

When we get inside his office at the top of the club, I don't even have a chance to glance around before he kicks the door shut with his foot and then turns around and slams my back against it.

He cups my face in his hands and stares down at me angrily. "What the fuck were you thinking?"

"I don't have to answer to you," I spit back at him angrily.

"Lacey," he growls as he gives my shoulders a little shake. "Don't leave your place without your phone ever again."

"Why?" I widen my eyes innocently before I accuse him, "So you can track me?"

His jaw hardens, and his eyes glitter dangerously. "So I can make sure you're safe."

"I can take care of my—" I don't even finish the word before Devon lets out an animalistic growl and then smashes his lips down onto mine.

I now know why I've been fighting him so hard. I think I knew it deep down all along. I knew that if his lips ever touched mine, it would completely wreck me. When Devon kisses me, I feel something snap into place inside of me. All of my protests vanish, and I can't remember the reason I've been fighting him. Why was I fighting this?

I turn to jelly, my body going lax against him. He wraps his arms around my back and pulls me flush against him.

I gasp when I feel his hard erection pressing into my stomach. I tremble at the length and girth of him. Good lord, he feels as big as my forearm. I might be a virgin, but I've seen porn before, so I know Devon is very well endowed.

He groans in the back of his throat, and I feel that groan reverberate throughout my own chest.

His arms tighten around me victoriously when I whimper into his mouth. I have no more defenses. He's completely destroying me with a kiss—so much so that tears bring to my eyes and roll down my cheeks.

He pulls back and wipes the tears away from my cheeks with the pads of his thumbs, shushing me as he does. "There we go as, baby. It's okay. Let it all out. I'm here now. I'm going to take care of you."

My tears only amplify when he croons such sweet words to me. I don't even know why I'm crying. I guess it's the sheer magnitude of all the emotions swirling through my mind.

"Devon, I...I—" My voice is shaky. My entire body is shaking. I try to speak but can't find the words I need to express what I'm feeling.

"I know," he reassures me. "I feel it too. There are no words. It's just us." He drops his forehead onto mine before he whispers again, "It's just us."

"Devon, this is crazy," I finally manage to get out.

He doesn't disagree with me. Instead, he looks deeply into my eyes as he repeats, "It's just *us*. It doesn't matter if it doesn't make sense. It doesn't matter what anyone thinks. Nothing matters except us. Me and you. Do you understand me?"

"What about work?" I don't know why my mind suddenly goes there, but he chuckles. "Lacey, I'm a billionaire. You don't have to work anymore."

"But—" I begin, but he shushes me with a finger to my lips.

"You're mine. I'm going to take care of you. If you

want to come into the office every day, then you're more than welcome. I love having you near me all the time so I can kiss and touch you whenever I want, but if you want to stay home and do nothing, that's fine, too."

"Home?" I ask with a raised eyebrow.

"Yes," His eyes become heated. "Our home. You're coming home with me. Where you belong."

My mind starts going a thousand miles a minute, but before I can fully process everything, he shuts down any of my further questions by kissing me again. He kisses me so deeply, this time thrusting his tongue in and out of my mouth in a blatant replication of the sexual act, leaving no doubt what he wants from me.

His hands are suddenly all over me, trailing down to reach the hem of my dress and then coming up to cup my ass cheeks.

He groans and thrusts his hardness against me, humping me through our clothes. The delicious friction sends snaps of pleasure shooting up from between my legs where he's hitting this spot that almost makes me feel ticklish, but it feels so good.

I can't stop the moan that tears up from my throat. That seems to encourage him because his humping only becomes wilder. "Do you see what you do to me, Lacey?" he rasps against my ear. "You make me lose control. Make me feel like coming in my pants. You know I haven't nutted since the day I first saw your face?"

I look up at him with wide eyes.

"That's right," he confirms. "I wasn't going to come until I could put it in between your sweet thighs where it's supposed to go."

Oh god, those words do something to me. I feel flushed all over and moisture pools between my thighs. "Devon," I whisper his name shakily.

"Let me worship you," he whispers against the column of my throat before he plants wet kisses all down it. My body moves with a mind of its own. I crane my neck to the side to give him greater access to my throat. When he sucks and bites on it, I know it's going to leave marks. I also know that's his intention because if I know anything about Devon by now, it's that not only is he tenacious when he wants something, but he's jealous and possessive. This man has decided that I'm his, and he's going to make sure the world knows it.

I'm tired of fighting it, and I can't help but feel flattered at the thought of being the object of his attention. If I'm being totally honest with myself, I think the real reason I ran from him for so long was because I didn't feel like I deserved it. I'm just an orphan no one's ever wanted. I can't believe that anyone could really want me the way he does, with such intensity. From day one, Devon has made his intentions clear. As impossible as it is to believe, he *wants* me. Badly.

It's in the way his lips slide over my collarbone and the swell of my breasts, my arms, and every inch of my skin. It's obvious in the way he drops kisses over every inch of me in between whispering words of love and passion against my heated skin.

I relax with a tiny sigh and finally give in, looping my arm around his neck.

Devon lifts his head back to capture my lips again, and I kiss him back this time, surrendering to his ardor.

CHAPTER EIGHT

Devon

I FEEL the moment Lacey submits to me fully. My chest swells with pride. *Finally.* "Yes," I whisper against her lips before I break away from them and rid her of her dress, leaving her in only that beautiful black bra-and-panty set.

I make quick work of pulling the cups of her bra down to expose the pretty little rosebuds of her breasts. I suck them into my mouth and swirl my tongue over them, loving the way she spears her little fingers through my hair as I suckle her.

I don't know if she's aware that she's even doing it,

but she's gyrating her hips against me, pumping me through my slacks.

With a strangled groan, I place a hand on her hips to still her, knowing that I'll come prematurely if she keeps doing that. "I'm going to have to get inside you soon before I burst, baby, but not before I taste what's finally mine." I trail kisses over her stomach as I drop to my knees before her and slowly peel her panties from her perfect body, revealing the most perfect pussy I've ever seen. I kiss it reverently and stroke its slick folds with my tongue.

My God, she's the sweetest thing I've ever tasted, and I can't get enough of her. "Taste like pure fucking sugar, honey," I whisper against her before I dive in and began eating her in earnest. It doesn't take long before I can tell she's on the brink of orgasm, and as much as I want her to come on my face, I want her first orgasm to be oh my cock.

"Have you ever orgasmed before, baby?" I ask her as I slow down my licking.

She lets out a frustrated whimper and shakes her head.

I growl at the confirmation, feeling like a caveman for being pleased at that knowledge that I'll be the first one to give her one. I want to be all her firsts. Her last. Her everything.

When I stand, she whimpers in protest, her voice breathy and her face flushed. "Why did you stop?"

I can't help the smug feeling that puffs out my chest, knowing I have her that desperate. "Because your first orgasm is going to be on my cock where it belongs," I tell her, my voice so husky it comes out rough and gritty.

I quickly shuck off my shirt and pants before removing her bra. I want us completely naked, skin on skin, nothing between us. Lacey hasn't asked about a condom, and thank fuck, because there's no way I'm using one with her. I never want anything between us. Not even a fucking rubber. She's mine, and I want to claim her in the most primitive way possible.

"You're so perfect, sweetheart," I tell her as I gather her up my arms and carry her over to my couch, where I spread her out before me. All I can do is just gaze at her for a moment. My cock is leaking, and I'll be surprised if I make it two pumps without coming inside her.

"You're mine," I tell her. She blushes as her eyes trail over my chest and legs before they settle on the appendage jutting out between my thighs. She bites her lips and turns worried eyes up to me.

"It'll fit," I promise her as I line my crown up with her hole and push gently into her. She tenses, and I suck on her nipples. When her body relaxes beneath me, I push further in. Every time she tenses up, I kiss her lips, her throat, her nipples, anywhere and every-where until she eventually softens enough for me to slide further inside her. Over and over again, we do this dance. I'm stretching her painstakingly slowly until I reach her hymen. I stop long enough to tilt her chin up and force her to look at me. "Look at me when I'm making you mine," I order her.

She bites her lip, but obediently keeps her eyes pinned on mine. I watch her eyes as I push through the barrier of her innocence, claiming her as mine. Victory roars in my chest as I slip into her tight heat. Lacey doesn't scream or cry out when I pop her cherry. Instead, she keeps her eyes locked on mine. Her breathing ticks up until it's coming out in shallow pants. I see the pinch of pain in her eyes as I seat myself fully inside her, but then I see the wonder at the new sensation. Her blue eyes are shimmering with all the emotions pulsing between us.

Her breath is coming out in pants as I stretch her little body wider than it's ever been before. She's grip-ping me tighter than a fist. Sweat breaks out on my brow as I concentrate on not spilling inside her too soon. "Are you okay?"

She expels a shaky breath before she nods and

wiggles her hips. My eyes roll back in my head, and my hand shoots out to grasp her hip and hold her still. My balls are so full they feel like they could overflow at any moment.

I speak through clenched teeth as I fight for control, "Fuck, you can't do that, baby. Not unless you want this to be over with before it's even begun."

She giggles, and I open my eyes to see her smiling up at me. I can't help but smile back. "Fuck, look at how beautiful you are impaled on my cock. You're going to kill me with that beautiful smile and that pretty little giggle."

"Devon," she whispers, her voice thick with emotion.

I flick my thumb over her nipple, and I feel her muscles clench around me. "Fuck," I curse before I finally snap. "Gotta move, sunshine."

And then it's out of my hands. My body takes over, and I rut into her primitively like a beast in heat. Lacey clings to me with her arms and legs wrapped around me. "That's it," I tell her. "Hold on to me. I've got you, baby. You want me to make you come?"

She moans, and I feel a tingle at the base of my spine. I suck her nipple into my mouth as I feel my release climbing up my stalk. All it takes is one swirl of my tongue around the bud before she tenses up.

"Devon!" she screams my name, and then she's fluttering around me wildly.

"Oh, fuck yes. I feel that little pussy falling open for me. Give it to me, baby. Yes, just like that." I don't know if she hears anything I'm saying to her. Her eyes roll back in her head, and she arches up into me an invitation I can't refuse.

I plunge into her heat one last time before my climax overtakes me. I spill into her so hard that I feel my own liquid heat surrounding my cock where it's still buried deep inside her. I come so much that it drips out of her and makes a mess on us on the couch, but I don't care. This is hands-down the most intense orgasm in my life, and I know it's not just because of my week-long abstinence waiting for her. It's just *her*. She does this to me.

"Mine," I croak out as a rush of possession floods my entire being. "You're mine, Lacey," I tell her as I stroke her hair and rain kisses down all over her face as I continue to jet thick ropes of sticky release inside her.

"I'm yours," I hear her sweet little voice say. My arms tighten around her back as I pull her against my chest and continue to spurt inside her.

I don't know how long we lie like that with my cock still seated deep inside her, me holding her in my arms, but I never want to be parted from her. I could stay like this forever.

She's the most precious thing in the world. The light in my darkness. I've found my sunshine, and I'm never letting her go.

EPILOGUE

Three Years Later

Lacey

I HAND a lollipop to the little girl before she leaves my office and I have a little chat with her mother, letting her know my professional opinion of how her daughter's therapy is coming along. With plenty of love and care, she'll be just fine. My heart swells when I see how concerned the mother is. This girl already has so much going for her. She has a mother who truly cares about her, and that's enough for now.

After the woman leaves, I tidy up until I hear the bell above my door jangle again. My heart softens when I see my husband carrying our two-year-old daughter on his shoulders.

"Mommy! Mommy!" she screams, holding her arms out for me. I take our little girl in my arms and smother her with kisses before I tilt my head up to accept a kiss from my husband.

Devon is amazing. He's no longer my boss. In fact, I never went back to work for him. That working for him stuff was just his bizarre way of getting me into his life so that he could put his moves on me anyway.

When he refused to release me and let me go back to my apartment, I didn't even try to fight it. With that one kiss, he wrecked me and stole my entire life. I let him move me in with him without protest and took him up on his offer to pay for me to go to college and pursue my dream career. Now I'm a child psychologist with my very own office that, of course, my husband funded.

While some people might turn up their nose up at me letting him pay for my career, I don't care. It's like Devon once said. It doesn't matter if anyone understands or what the world thinks. We're just us, and we're all the matters. Us and our baby girl."

"Are you ready to see Linda?" I ask our baby girl.

"Linda! Linda!" she screams her babysitter's name and claps her hands excitedly. I smile. I love that our baby girl loves her babysitter. While Devon and I both try to spend as much time with our daughter as we can, we also schedule at least one night a week for just us, and tonight is that night.

I can already see the promises in Devon's eyes every time his gaze rakes over me. They tell me that my husband has a night of sex in store for me. He looks like he's going to pounce on me at any moment.

In fact, we don't even make it out of my office. No sooner does Linda, who also works as my secretary, take our baby girl out for some ice cream, does Devon lock the door of my office, draw the shades, and push me up against the wall. He pulls my skirt up roughly. "Been thinking about this pussy all day," he groans as he kisses my mouth while pushing my panties to the side.

He's already pulled his cock out, and he's inside me in one hard thrust.

I moan at the sudden penetration. It doesn't matter how many times we have sex or the fact that I had a baby. I still struggle to take all of my husband's length and girth. He still stretches me impossibly wide and makes me feel fuller than I ever could have imagined, and I love it.

I wrap my arms and legs around him as he picks me up and fucks me furiously against the wall. "This pussy has been aching for my cock all day, hasn't it?" he prompts me.

I already know what he wants, so I give it to him. Moisture pools between my thighs as I get more turned on, too. "Yes, I've been waiting for you to breed me," I speak right against his ear.

"Fuck," he stutters out. "I'm going to put another baby up inside you tonight, sweetheart. I promise you that. I've been saving up this big nut just for you, sweet wife."

"Oh god!" His filthy talk sets me off. Without warning, I'm orgasming, coming so hard around him it takes my breath away.

My release must trigger his because he buries his head in my neck and roars as he rides out his own release, jutting his hips up into mine. I feel his hot cum spurting up inside me and branding me with his liquid heat until it drips down my thighs.

That's another thing about my husband. He comes like a racehorse, always making a sticky mess of us. It's no wonder I got pregnant as soon as I did with him busting big loads like this inside me.

He kisses my lips sweetly as we both float back down to earth. "I love you, sunshine," he tells me as he runs a hand through my hair.

I smile back at him contentedly. "I love you too, stalker."

He smirks at me smugly, as always completely unapologetic.

My billionaire stalker.

THE END

Emma Bray writes intense, steamy romances with possessive alpha males who'll stop at nothing to claim the women they want. Emma's insta-love stories are filled with heat, passion and happily ever afters. Visit Emma's website to get a FREE book: www.authoremmabray.com.